Tales from a Sick Bed

Also by L.P. Howarth published by Catnip

Bodyswap: The Boy who was 84
Tales from a Sick Bed: Brainstorms
Tales from a Sick Bed: The Medicine Chest

Tales
from a
Sick Bed

fever Dreams

L. P. HOWARTH

CATNIP BOOKS
Published by Catnip Publishing Ltd
14 Greville Street
London EC1N 8SB

This edition first published 2009
1 3 5 7 9 10 8 6 4 2

A CIP catalogue record for this book is available from the British Library.

ISBN 978 1 846470 82 0

Printed in Poland

www.catnippublishing.co.uk

Contents

It's a
Fever Dream

You know when you're off school and ill in bed, and everything seems kind of large and nightmarish – when feverish thoughts invade your brain, and you're not sure where they came from?

You're off school – score. But you're ill in bed. You've been dragged to the doctor. You're hot – very hot. The comics and sweets beside the bed look unreal, and anyway it's far too much effort to reach them. Unbelievably, you haven't been hungry for three days. Downstairs, Mum plugs the kettle in and chats to her regional boss. Soon she'll go out with her case of lipsticks and eyeshadows, ringing doorbells and chanting 'Avalon

Calling'. You drift off to sleep and in your dreams the doorbell rings, and a strange version of a cosmetics representative stands on the doorstep, selling you very strange things…

Evening, and Dad's in, eating his warmed-up tea. The telly burbles downstairs, and the cat's come to sit on your chest. You don't really want its death-breath in your face, but come to think of it, you don't really like the look of that fluffy snake under the door, either. It's supposed to be stopping draughts. In reality it's stopping the air coming in, and its glassy eye knows what it's doing. Dad – I'm suffocating! Dad! After a while, you drift off again, and this time the draught excluder snakes into your dreams in a way you never imagined.

Morning, and the clatter of breakfast downstairs reminds you you're still not hungry. So does the congealing boiled egg beside the bed.

'Where's my violin music?' your sister moans, in the hall. 'I left it in my bag, and now it's gone. There's millions and millions of lost things in the world.' You can hear her tipping her bag out. 'Where do they all GO?'

The door slams behind her, and all the lost things in the universe whirl around in your mind, all the lost socks, library books, pens, string, bus passes and coins, umbrellas, buttons, wallets, ties, passports, all the homework you ever lost or meant to lose, spinning away into space, and massing into a planet winking with pen tops and batteries, torches, fifty pence pieces and hair slides. And you know that the lost things can't help it, that something has brought them there, that it's really not their fault . . .

Some things are just too big to carry around inside you all day. The whole thing with Mum and Dad, your brother leaving for uni, it's just too heavy.

That's when the headaches hit. You like things to stay the same. That's what Queen of the Smooth does.

'You don't want to go saying anything about the Queen of the Smooth.' Your dad warns.

You know she's a fever dream. But she takes up the tangles inside your mind and kind of smooths 'em out. Trouble is, you'll always need her. Unless someway, somehow, the tangles ever come undone...

Evening again, and you're well enough to watch a horror film and snack on dry Shreddies in place of crisps. After a while, you're glad there's no crisps. Some scenes are pretty gross. Squinting through a Shreddie allows you to screen things out.

Fever Dreams

'What on earth are you doing?' Mum asks, when she looks in.

Blocking out the bits I don't want to see?

By looking through breakfast cereal?

Nutritious malted squares packed with vitamins, you correct her. You should try it sometime.

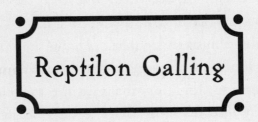

Reptilon Calling

Inez says, 'Gimme the remote.'

'You're sitting on it.' Sam Frost isn't about to hand it over. She isn't about to do anything she doesn't *have* to. It's Saturday, why should she?

'It's over there. Right by your foot. Are you going to pass it over or what?'

Sam Frost yawns. She passes the TV remote to her sister with an exaggerated effort, like she's lifting a deadweight or something.

'*In* your own time.' Inez snatches it, switching channels crossly.

Saturday morning TV flickers over the fish tank and

the coffee table, over Sam and Inez Frost, over the neat front room Mum expects them to leave as they found it, whenever she's out at work, which she is, this Saturday morning, over Iggy the iguana's cage on the floor in his dust-tray in the corner. Iggy stirs inside. His eyes mirror the front room, the girls, the telly, the morning, then blink away into his skull cavity as he swallows. Other than this, he hardly moves a muscle. Through the fish-tank on the windowsill above Iggy, no one – except nosy Nora Knebworth next door – no one, especially not the fishes, notices the slim green car pulling up outside.

Out of the slim green car steps a sharp-shouldered suit with stiff red hair and an *attitude*. Dressed in green from head to foot – green suit, green shirt, green shoes – he's seventeen, maybe eighteen, tops. He flips open the boot and unpacks a case or two. He consults a list. Then he snaps down the boot and looks around.

'Get me a bowl of Weetos?' Inez looks appealing. 'I got *you* some yesterday. Sammie-the-Spam. *Please*.'

'Get 'em yourself.' Sam folds her arms on the settee. 'Sammie-the-*not*-Spam, I think.'

'You're only not spammy if you get 'em.'

'You wish.'

Reptilon Calling

'You're nearest the kitchen. Please.'

The doorbell rings. Sam and Inez Frost watch the
It's Saturday! cook-off as Our Resident Chef pours
two-step chocolate icing over Easy Butter Fudge Cakes.
Check website for recipe. No need for parental
supervision. Then it's time for *Madhouse*. Sam and Inez
watch *Madhouse* contestants battling it out over a pool
of bright blue gunge. The doorbell rings again. Someone
falls in the gunge. Last Man Alive is the next game. No
gunge pool in Last Man Alive.

'Isn't that the doorbell?' Inez says at last. This time it
rings between rounds.

'Great.' Sam Frost sits up crossly. 'A Saturday morning
lie-in with no hassles – *not.'*

'You shouldn't answer it, anyway,' Inez says, lazily.
'You never know who it might be.'

The doorbell rings loudly, insistently.

'Probably an axe-murderer,' Inez guesses.

'The milkman.'

'Someone selling something.'

'Nora Knebworth, more like.'

'Ignore it,' Inez says.

'Whoever it is'll hear the telly.'

'So?'

'So, they'll know we're in.'

'So why don't you answer it?'

'I *am*.' Sam Frost gets up irritably. The doorbell rings again. 'It might be Paul – or Danny. Can't *you* go? I'm not going in my pyjamas.'

'Get your dressing-gown, then.'

'You.'

'You're nearest the door.'

'Oh, right. I do everything *my whole life*, just 'cos I'm nearest the door.'

Sam Frost flounces out and crams on a jumper and jeans. A minute later she's out in the hall discerning a shape through the door. A sharp-shouldered shape that sees she sees him perfectly well through the figured frosted glass.

'Yes?' she calls. 'Who is it?'

'Reptilon calling!' the voice sings, as if it's bringing light and air into everyone's lives like some kind of miracle cleaner. A card appears through the door. 'Mrs Frost's regular call?'

'Are you selling cleaning things or something?'

'No style, no *way*.' The sharp-shouldered shape shrugs off the very *idea*. 'Could *you* stand to sell that stuff?'

The voice is friendly. Young. Kind of on-*your*-side

already. Sam Frost picks up the card. A classy-looking green card. A green card that says: *Anthony Omnivore: Your Reptilon Representative*, with a picture of Anthony Omnivore on one side, and *Reptilon – Cold-Bloodedly the Best* on the other.

'Can you call back later?' Sam asks. *Anthony Omnivore.* What kind of a name is that? 'Mum's ou – Mum's busy right now.'

The shape outside says, 'Can I just leave you her order?'

'Her order?'

'There's a free CD with orders over ten pounds, this month only. If I have to take it away again, she's going to miss out on her gift.'

Sam hesitates.

'I'm only thinking of Mrs Frost,' the shape continues. It swaps feet. It looks like it's got red hair. 'I can't really leave her order out on the step, you know what I mean?'

Sam thinks a moment then opens the door. Anthony Omnivore winks. He's very pale, very thin, very young – very quick, in a jerky sort of way. In quick, jerky movements he's in at the door with a box of something-or-other, jerkily sizing up rooms like he knows where he's going, jerkily nudging open the living-room door with the box – a big, green, shiny box – before Sam has time to register the free CD he hands her as he comes in. Sam follows the green suited rep with the *very* red hair down the hall and into the living room where Inez stands, flushed, in her nightie. Sam looks down at her free CD. *Monster*, by REM. She watches the rep as he sets down his box. He seems to know just where to put it.

'Anthony Omnivore. Reptilon Cosmetics.'

He extends a hand to Inez. Inez Frost stares back. Anthony Omnivore's shirt is green, Anthony Omnivore's suit and shoes and socks, are green. Even his *fingernails* are green.

'Hi,' she says, 'I'm just going.' And makes a dash for the door.

Mr Reptilon takes in the room. He especially takes in Iggy 'Nice iguana.' Mr Reptilon nods.

'When he's behaving himself,' Sam eyes Iggy fondly.

Iggy's doing his 'threatened' display. He's sensed an intruder in the room. Sam lifts him out and soothes him. She puts him down on the cheesy wickerwork shelving unit, his favourite spot for display, where he clicks and bristles and eyes Mr Reptilon savagely. Sam eyes him, too. She supposes he has Mum's order form. Or, at least, some proof of purchase.

'So is it all paid for, Mr Omnivore –'

'Tony.'

'I mean, I didn't know Mum had make-up from –'

'Reptilon.' Tony likes saying it, anyone can see. 'More than just make-up. Cold-bloodedly the Best.'

'Right. So what's in the box?'

'He's territorial, he is.' Ignoring Sam's question, Tony taps Iggy all down the length of his body with the tips of his long green nails. 'You want to find him a mate.' He fans out his nails for Sam Frost. 'Like this shade? *Everglades*. I've got it in pearlised as well.'

'Did Mum order nail varnish?'

'And the rest.' Tony picks Iggy up. Iggy stiffens and hisses. 'Hiss at me, will you?' Tony smiles, but his smile isn't warm. 'Not many people keep iguanas these days. Mind if I ask you for a coffee?'

Inez reappears in dress and jumper to boggle some more at Anthony Omnivore. She follows him into the kitchen, where Sam's hurriedly making instant coffee, chatting to Tony all the time. Sam isn't hurrying because she wants to get rid of Tony: she's hurrying because she doesn't want to keep Tony waiting. Already they're on first-name terms. Sam finds him easy to talk to. Inez watches Tony closely. Tony has a stiff neck. He turns his head when he looks at Inez. He doesn't move his eyes. He doesn't look at her often. Mainly he looks at Sam. Inez can't say she likes him. She can't say she *doesn't* like him, either.

Then something happens she doesn't expect. Inez sees Tony – Sam doesn't – snatch something out of the air with a movement sharp as a knife. Before Sam turns he brings up his hand – Inez's eyes are on stalks – and pops a fly into his mouth. He turns his neck to look at her. Inez swallows and looks away. *Still* he isn't dislikeable.

Sam turns at last. 'Black or white?'

'White, thanks – I like milk.' Tony's quick bright eyes take in everything – the black-and-white tiled floor, the cheery bowls on the table, the toaster with Smiley stickers over it, even the crusty bowl of catfood on the floor. Especially he notices the cereal-packet dinosaurs lining the windowsill like they meant to get out, some day.

Quick as a snake, he picks one up. 'Nice lizards.'

'Free with Chocopops.' Sam Frost hands Tony his coffee. 'Took us ages to get them all.'

Tony examines the plastic stegosaurus. 'Look better painted. I got just the thing for these.'

18

Back in the living room he flips open his case, unfolding it three ways to lay out a glittering wad of nail varnishes. Neatly sheathed bottles of nail polish, from gunmetal grey through metallic purples and greens to silver and gold lie exposed like a surgeon's kit.

'Cool colours.' Inez says. They *are* cool colours. Inez can't help herself.

'The Gilded Lizard range.' Tony grins. He loves 'em. 'Perfect for painting models. I use 'em all the time.'

'Why are they Gilded Lizards?'

'See these testers?' Tony picks out a bottle and hands it to Inez. 'See they look like lizards? Brilliant colours. Give 'em a go. Try whatever you like.'

Sam and Inez want to. But first they take a look. The nail polish Tony hands over has a gold lizard's head for a top. Shade 42, says the label, *Fabulous Basilisk*. Now that Inez looks at it, she sees how fabulous it is. The colour inside the bottle winks from green to blue, the way a peacock's feather does. Each Gilded Lizard is different. They even have gem-studded eyes.

'They're nice,' she says, 'aren't they, Sam?'

'I use 'em for badges as well as my nails.' Tony opens *Fabulous Basilisk* for Inez. 'High-performance metallics. It's really good gear – you should try some.'

Fever Dreams

The girls don't need too much persuading. Iggy the iguana watches unblinkingly from the top of the telly as Sam and Inez frost their nails with one brilliant colour after another.

'Iggy, get back in your cage.' Carefully, Sam lifts him down, and puts him back in his cage.

'Don't smudge your nails.'

'I haven't.'

It's Saturday! is over, lunchtime sports just beginning. Warmed by the telly, Iggy brings up his crest. Tony cracks open more and more bottles of nail varnish. Sam and Inez get into it. As fast as Tony fields them, Gilded Lizard testers and matching lip-pencils, mascaras and eye-liners swap hands and litter the floor. The colours are extraordinary Mrs Frost's order is well and truly forgotten as more and more compartments of Tony's case open out.

'You can't see the colours in this light.' Tony gets up jerkily. 'Mind if I draw the curtains?' Sam and Inez aren't listening. They've never seen anything like the Gilded Lizard range in their life. Tony draws the curtains. The cricket scores come on. Iggy's eyes blaze gold and green – all the colours of Reptilon.

Sam Frost outlines her eyes in front of the living-room mirror. The telly lights up her face. How long has she been standing there? Half an hour? An hour? Longer? All of a sudden it seems like a long time has passed. *'How long have we been doing this?'* Sam Frost whispers to Inez. *'I'm cold. Do you feel cold?'*

Tony hears them. 'Here. Feel my hand.'

'You're freezing.' Inez says, freezing herself.

'Always am.' Tony laughs. 'I'm cold-blooded, me.' He takes out a gorgeously packaged box. 'You know what they say – cold hands, warm heart. Like to try some foundation?'

It's Inez's turn at the mirror. She's moving slower and slower. She smoothes on some foundation. It slips on easily, like the kind of silky mud you can barely feel. She can hardly be bothered to smooth it on properly. She smoothes it on any old way. Sam examines her lipstick in Tony's demonstration-pack mirror. Her lips are purple-blue to match her arms. Her arms feel cold and heavy. Sam feels really drowsy. 'I'm tired,' she says. 'I want to lie down.'

The rep smiles broadly. Was that a forked-looking tongue? 'Not before you've tried the foundation, surely.'

Inez stares at her reflection. Slowly she turns. 'I tried some already. What do you think?' She smiles. She has blue lips and red eyes. The skin over which she's applied *Reptilon Slime Plus Foundation* is completely green and scaly.

'Her eyes . . .' Sam says faintly, 'her skin . . .'

'Those red contact lenses *kill* me, don't they kill you?' The rep rubs his hands together drily. His claw-like nails seem to have grown. 'Looks fabulous, doesn't she? Scaly. Cold. Green. *Absolutely lovely.*'

Sam lies down on the settee. Inez lies down beside Sam. The light from the telly flickers over them, this time an ad for Monster Munch. 'I don't feel too good.' Inez complains. 'Move over, will you? I want to have a sleep.'

'*Sleep then, why don't you?*' hisses the rep. He waits a moment. '*Sleep.*' He puts away his things and snaps up the lock on his case. He looks at Sam and Inez, asleep and green on the settee. '*You're beautiful, you know that?*'

The front door closes softly. A green car pulls away outside. No one but nosy Nora Knebworth next door notices it go. In the next hour or so, the iguana on top of the telly changes position only twice. The warmth makes it sleepy. It lets its tail hang down.

Racing from Newbury, then golf, then highlights of the third Test against Pakistan. A fly buzzes the screen, then bumbles away to get trapped between the curtains and the window. The curtains aren't quite closed. Through the fish tank on the windowsill, a heavily loaded estate, with shopping inside it, is visible – mainly to Nora Knebworth – pulling up outside. Mrs Frost jumps out of it. She slams the door, gets out her key, hurries up the path.

'Girls!' Mrs Frost jams her key in the front door crossly. 'Girls, I've got the shopping! Can't you open this door?'

Mrs Frost gets two full carrier bags around the door with difficulty and sets them down in the kitchen. After she's unpacked a few items, she crosses the hail. 'Girls, are you there? I could do with a hand unpacking.' She pushes the living-room door 'What's going on in here? Why are the curtains half closed?'

Mrs Frost rips back the curtains. The iguana on top of the telly rolls up its eyes. Its tail hangs down over the screen. 'Iggy! What are you doing out of your cage?' Mrs Frost snatches him up. 'What on earth—'

The shiny green box in the middle of the room takes her by surprise. *Thank you for your order*, says the order-form on the front. *With compliments from Reptilon Cosmetics.*

'What on earth's been going on, Iggy? What's this box on the floor? What d'you think you're doing on the telly?'

The iguana never has much chance of answering because Mrs Frost starts back and almost drops it, the moment she sees that Iggy the iguana is, in fact, *still safely in his cage*. At the same time as she steps back, she brings down her hand on a *third* iguana on the back of the settee. 'Ugh!' she says, and catches her breath, shoving down the first, like it's poison.

'You got your delivery, then.'

Mrs Frost spins round 'Oh. Nora. Hello.'

'I *did* knock.' Nosy Nora Knebworth comes right in. 'I expect you didn't hear me.' She nudges the box on the floor with her foot. The green, shiny box Mrs Frost has yet to open. 'They make a nice job of it, don't they?'

'What delivery?' Mrs Frost asks. 'What are you talking about?'

'Reptilon called. I saw his green car.'

'What's Reptilon when it's at home?'

'It's a cosmetics company.' Nora Knebworth explains. 'Make-up in boxes like lizards. I've seen the rep before. Funny-looking article. Bit like a lizard himself.'

Reptilon Calling

'Have you seen Sam and Inez?' Mrs Frost looks around vaguely, as though Sam and Inez are about to jump out from under a cushion and say, 'Surprise!'

Instead she sees iguanas. The iguana she dropped in disgust looks up at her stupidly. Mrs Frost does a double-take. The iguana in the cage is definitely Iggy. The one she just dropped isn't. It's a funny thing to come home to. Iguanas all over the place. Iggy in his cage – another Iggy on the telly – and *another* iguana on the back of the settee. That makes *three iguanas and no girls*. Mrs Frost's heart starts hammering. Iggy plus *two iguanas that weren't there before*. What on earth is she thinking about? What on earth is going on?

'We *did* have one,' she says distractedly, 'now there's *three*. I don't know where they're all coming from.'

'Three what?'

'Iguanas. Do they breed when you've only got one? Sam! Inez! Where are you?'

'They must be in the house,' says nosy Nora Knebworth. 'They didn't go out, I've been watching, I mean, I'd have noticed, if they'd gone out.'

Mrs Frost examines a pool of something green in the carpet. She pushes it with her finger. 'Nail varnish.' She frowns.

'Funny-looking things, aren't they?' Nora Knebworth sits down on the settee. The iguanas stare past her. They never even blink. 'Look at them watching the telly,' she says. 'You'd think they understood. Aren't you going to open it, then?'

'Open what?'

'Your order.'

Mrs Frost squats to examine her box. She unties the silver-green ribbon on top. She reads the order-form. *With compliments from Reptilon Cosmetics.* She looks at the iguanas. Two *extra* iguanas. She reads the order-form again. It's in the name of Sam and Inez Frost. At the bottom it says: *Shed that Skin and Discover a New You.*

Something about the front room, the telly, the morning makes Mrs Frost's blood run cold. Slowly she opens the box. *It doesn't matter what's in it*, the two *extra* iguanas' eyes tell her, coldly. *The box was never the point.* She gets up and goes out again.

Mrs Frost shouts in the hall. She thinks – she hopes – she hears someone upstairs.

'Girls!' she calls. 'I'm coming up! Girls! I'm waiting – *Where are you?*'

The Excluder

Gran Dodd's house was roomy and cold. Whenever they visited Gran Dodd's house, Rob and Emma Gifford wore at least two sweaters apiece. It didn't stop them shivering upstairs. No matter how many heaters she gave them, Gran Dodd had no idea just how cold a hand playing Auto Theft Three could become. Plus the thing under the door was no help.

Robbie and Em never *had* liked the sneaky-eyed stuffed snake that lay – or used to – under the doors at Gran Dodd's house. Gran called it an *excluder*, because it excluded, or blocked out, the draughts. Green with orange spots and a nasty, damp-feeling body, they'd had the strangest feeling it mainly excluded *them*. It had always eyed them nastily, up to and including the time Em had taken fright, aged five, and howled until the snake had been put away. It had sat in a cupboard under Gran Dodd's stairs getting greener and damper for years, and the draught had scoured under the doors until Gran had got a sausage dog to block it, but ages ago *that* had gone, too. Nothing had replaced the orange-and-green snake after that, and no one remembered it much. But now it was back again – *big* time.

Em eyed the excluder nervously. Skirting the living-room door – *hate* you, you evil-eyed door-snake – she wondered why Gran had washed it and put it on show. Greener and oranger, *eviller*, somehow, than ever Emma Gifford remembered it, it lay beside the living-room door with a crummy-looking smile on its face. It had lain in the cupboard for years. Why had it come out now?

Rejoining Gran in the kitchen, Emma remembered to ask. 'You know that snake?'

'What snake?'

'That stuffed snake by the door.'

'You mean the old draught excluder?' Gran Dodd smiled. 'D'you know, I found that old snake in the cupboard the other day, and I thought, Emma will remember this. You used to play with that snake –'

No, I didn't, Emma thought.

'– and pretend it was chasing you till Grandpa had to put it away, remember?'

'The thing is –' The thing is, Emma wanted to say, the thing is, I never liked it. I *never* used to play with that snake. You've remembered it all wrong, Gran. Instead, she said: 'The thing is, it could be dangerous.'

'Dangerous, lovey? Why's that?'

'Someone might trip over it. You might forget it's there.'

'I haven't fallen headlong over a draught excluder in sixty-three years, so far.'

'I think we should put it away again. We don't really need it, anyway.'

'Well, now,' Gran Dodd had a way of not hearing things she didn't agree with, 'well now, let me see – have you chopped up the apples?'

Gran Dodd and Em were making blackberry-and-apple jelly together. They made it together every year. A visit to Gran Dodd was good fun when Dad was away, even better at blackberry-jelly time. Robbie didn't always think so, but then Robbie could cycle down town with his mates, which is what Robbie usually did. He didn't understand – never would – the blackberry-jelly thing. That's what he'd said to Emma the night before.

'I don't get it,' he said.

'Get what?'

'The blackberry-jelly thing.'

'There's nothing to get,' Emma told him. 'It's just doing the same thing at the same time every year, with Gran Dodd, is all it is.'

'Right,' said Robbie. 'Fun City.'

Already they'd picked the blackberries. Now they'd be washed and stewed with apples. Then the mash would be strained overnight so that only the juice remained, to be boiled up, next day, with sugar.

The smell filling the house was the best thing – a musky, hedgerow smell of hot fruit with witchy, autumnal overtones never to be recaptured until the same time, the same ritual, next year. Every year the pillowcase full of blackberry mash hung dripping over a basin in the bath, revolving slowly, looking heartstoppingly like bloody pig's head or something. Every year it brought with it a flood of other September-time memories of doing the *same things at the same time* in exactly the same kind of way. Life had a rhythm at

The Excluder

Gran's. It wasn't all bump and jump and what's next, and oh-no-what-have-I-forgotten. That was what was nice about it – what Robbie, who didn't *get* life at Gran's – what Robbie would never understand.

After the blackberries had been stewed with the apples and the mash had been hung in the bathroom and the long, slow drip of blackberry juice, dark as blood, had started in the basin, Em played a long time with Rats. Rats was Gran's black-and-white cat. Really his name was Ratchet, because while still a kitten he'd learned to undo the ratchet on the summer-house door, where Gran had first kept him, and escape. So Ratchet, Gran had named him. But Em – always had – called him Rats.

Rats was soft and pliant, and went especially bendy whenever you turned him upside down so he stretched himself out unfeasibly long, which Emma did quite a lot. Rats wasn't coarse and bony, like the kittens that lived next door. Next door's kittens were rangy and hard-feeling with faces that looked all wrong. Rats was softer 'n all of 'em, and that was the nice thing about him. *Hard* kittens weren't the best, in Emma's opinion.

'Wonder what Dad's doing?' Robbie said, later that evening.

Gran said, 'Probably having a whale of a time.'

'Bet he isn't,' Robbie said, darkly. 'Bet he's falling off his windsurfer right now.'

'Dad's useless at windsurfing,' Em said.

'He's useless at most water-sports. That's why he went on a water-sports holiday.' Robbie added, sarcastically. Robbie was bitter about the water-sports. It was the first holiday Dad had had in years. But he couldn't let Dad go without him.

Gran said, 'A break will do him the world of good. A change is as good as a rest.'

'Makes a change not going to Mum's when Dad's away. I *like* staying here with you and making jelly.' She really meant it. Emma hugged Gran Dodd.

'Suck-up,' Robbie whispered.

'I like you liking staying.' Gran Dodd meant it, too. 'How's the time going on? Like to go up to bed now?'

'We usually stay down to see *Policewatch*.'

'Do you, dear? It's late.'

'Usually we stay up however long we want to on weekends,' Robbie said, louder than he had to. 'Usually I watch telly in bed and so does Em in her room.'

'I hope Dad wears a life-jacket,' Em worried, briefly.

'I'm sure it's all arranged.'

The Excluder

'He isn't exactly Mr Safety First. You know what he's like,' Em said.

'I know what he's like,' Gran agreed.

Later, upstairs and about to enter her small and well-loved bedroom at Gran Dodd's house, Emma stepped back in dismay. The snake – the excluder – had appeared or been placed, when she hadn't asked for it, beside her bedroom door. Probably Gran had put it there because she thought she liked it. Em stepped over it quickly, noticing, possibly for the first time, how very *pointed* was its expression, how very *wide* its mouth, how very *sinuous* its body. Horrible thing, Em thought. It'd be good if it had an accident. An accident might be arranged.

In the meantime, the excluder eyed her with its dim button eyes from the shadows under the door. Em considered asking Gran to remove it, but she thought that might make her look silly. It *was* silly that she couldn't – wouldn't – pick it up and move it herself. Very silly. But still. She nudged the excluder into position with her slipper. It might as well block out the draught, now that it was here. She really, really, *really* didn't want to touch it.

Thoughtfully, Em got undressed. Her back prickled all the time, as though the excluder were watching her.

She whipped around. It *was* watching her. She threw a T-shirt at it, but somehow missed entirely. It felt stupid to try again, so she hurriedly got into bed. Her eyes returned to the excluder again and again. Draughts under the doors *upstairs* were mainly non-existent. What did it think it was excluding? It wasn't worth feeling angry about. It was only a stuffed strip of jumble-sale-smelling fabric. How could she let a smelly old sausage from under the stairs get to her so badly? For all she cared, it could lie there and niff all night. It really was gruesome – who'd made it? Not Gran Dodd herself, Emma hoped. Who, in their worst nightmare, had sewn the excluder's horrible orange spots onto its horrible bright-green body? Had they *decided* on orange and green? Bought it specially? Used up scraps? Been colour-blind from birth? Probably it had been made by Auntie Hetty or Auntie Joan or maybe Mrs Bacon, Gran's friend, who made hats no one liked but everyone had to put up with. Em wished whoever'd made it had kept it to line the bin. With its sick-making colours it'd blend in with rubbish pretty well. Who'd know the difference if they saw it?

Emma snapped on her bedside light and took the first juicy *Celebrity Homes* off the pile of magazines she'd brought upstairs from the living room. An essential part of the Gran Dodd experience, it was funny the way they sucked you in, despite a feeling they shouldn't. What *Celebrity Homes* did was suck out your brains and leave you feeling disgusted. With its photo-spreads of luxury bedrooms it was a bit like nosing through someone else's house without having to say you were sorry. It *was* nosing through someone else's house without having to –

Em looked up. It was a funny thing, but the – the excluder looked different, somehow. Something to do with its beady button eyes catching the light at a different angle. Or maybe the kinks in its body. Em counted the kinks, so she'd know. *Five* bends in the snaky excluder's body, where the horrible green fabric wrinkled and the horrible orange spots got swallowed in puckers, plus a tail that stuck out at an angle, made its position pretty memorable. OK. All right. Check it out.

Em returned to *Celebrity Homes*. She could feel herself getting sleepy This was the very room – the very bed – she'd lain in to read Gnid Blyton when she was six, maybe seven. Only when she'd been reading the sinister-sounding Gnid for two or three years had she realized that her favourite reads were, in fact, written by a woman named Enid, not the *Gnid* of the scribbled signature.

Fever Dreams

Somehow it had taken the magic away, and she'd stopped reading Gnid altogether. Dopey, or what? Em smiled, remembering. On the other side of the wall, Robbie would be watching telly in bed. He got angry if he couldn't. Em wished he'd make an effort to be less angry with Dad, with Gran, with himself – with everything – for Gran's sake. Maybe tomorrow she'd sort him out. He needed sorting badly. Tomorrow she and Gran would make blackberry-and-apple jelly to the time-honoured recipe in the cookbook, the way they did every year. Together they would pour the fragrant, blood-heavy juice that had collected overnight in the basin in the bath, into a pan. They would heat it up and add sugar, and then they'd bring it all to a rolling boil – Em loved that phrase, to a *rolling boil* – and then the ticklish business of *getting a set* would begin.

'Rats, is that you?' Emma stirred in bed. She sat up, blinking, the headachy light by the bed reminding her that she must have fallen asleep without turning it off. A pile of *Celebrity Homes* slewed noisily on to the floor. Em woke up more fully. She sat up, suddenly on edge. Something – what? – had woken her up. It must be – was it Rats that had just moved by the door?

'*Rats. I know you're there.*'

The Excluder

It would've been good if it'd been an adventure story by Gnid. It would've been funny, if had happened to somebody else. As it was, it was just plain scary. Em tried not to make it obvious she'd noticed. Its button eyes looked deceptively dim. But there could be no doubt about it this time. The five kinks in its body had melted to two. It had straightened significantly and angled away from the door. *This time the excluder had moved.*

It's moved, but no one's moved it. A pulse beat high in Em's heart. *It's moved but no one's moved it, it's moved but no one's —*

She got up and jumped out of bed.

— moved it, it's moved but no one's —

She'd have to hurdle the snake with the all-seeing eyes to get out of the door, but the snake with the all-seeing eyes was the reason she wanted to leave. Plus, it knew she was on to it now.

— moved it — YET IT'S MOVED —

It had always had it in for her. It wasn't blocking draughts out at all. Instead, it was *blocking her in.* The excluder was excluding her — just as she'd always been afraid it would when she was little. The excluder was *excluding her from the rest of the house.*

Fever Dreams

IT'S MOVED AND NO ONE'S MOVED IT –

A special thrill of danger connected the snake with Emma's toes. The floor felt electric between them. There was no going back, now that it knew that she knew. No playing dumb or not noticing. The floor was a dangerous place. Now or never. Get out.

Surprisingly athletic for someone half asleep, Emma Gifford sprang neatly out of her bedroom and over the landing and fetched up, panting, in the bathroom. Nothing had nipped her ankles in passing. Nothing had seized her feet. The moonlight flooded in and showed her her toes. They were all there. Nothing had tried to get them. Nothing vaguely snake-like had pursued her. Backing against the bath, she sat down suddenly into it. Something wet and heavy brushed her face. Something nightmarishly like a hanged man – or a ham or a hanged ham or both – dolefully nudged her shoulder. She put out her hands to get up. Something complicated-feeling, wet, with edges involving a chair and a bowl made getting up a puzzle. *Where was she? What was happening?* Emma didn't care. Putting her hand – both hands – into the cold-and-bloody-whatever-it-was involved with the chair and the basin, she clambered out of the bath and out of the bathroom.

The Excluder

Bruised and cold, unsure whether she was asleep or awake, longing only for bed and knowing, dimly, there was some good reason she couldn't go back there, Emma sat hunched on the stair. She leaned her head against the wall – a nice, safe, uncomplicated wall, that wouldn't mind her sleeping against it if she wanted. After what seemed like a long time, Robbie touched her shoulder.

'Emma?'

'Blackit? On?'

'*Emma*. What are you doing?'

'Robbie – rollingboilofjuice – RatsGnid – I don't like it –'

'You're talking rubbish. Get up and go back to bed.'

'Ing a min.'

'No, now. Emma. Just *do* it, will you?'

Some time after Robbie had gone to the toilet and then back to bed, Emma finally got up. Hooking the draught excluder out of the way with the soap-rack she found in the bathroom, she stripped off her strangely soaked nightie and sank into bed.

The green-and-orange spotted snake eyed Emma Gifford in bed. Its view included a scattered pile of magazines, a knocked-over bedside light and a heap of tousled hair that included, somewhere under it, the face of Emma Gifford, fast asleep. Over the bed and the carpet – over the door-snake itself – the mark of blood was heavy. Robbie noticed it straightaway, the moment he opened the door.

'Em – oh, *what*? What *happened*?'

He looked around in horror. It was pretty early and he probably shouldn't wake her, but this was a case for –

'*Gran! Gran! Come here!*'

The excluder watched Robbie rush out. It could block out draughts, but it couldn't block out the morning, and all that it would bring to Emma Gifford. Everyone – Robbie and Gran – who came to see what was up would tread on the button-eyed snake. The excluder was used to that. It lay under doors. That was its job. The door-snake smiled its smile anyway.

'*Gran!*' Robbie shouted '*Get up! Emma's killed the cat!*'

Gran Dodd got up slowly. 'Robbie – is that you?'

'Yes, and I want you to come. It's Emma. Can you come *quickly*?'

Gran Dodd opened her door. 'Now then,' she said, 'what's up?'

The Excluder

'She was sitting on the stairs last night,' Robbie babbled, 'and I *thought* she looked a bit soggy but I went back to bed and now *Rats* is gone –'

Gran Dodd did up her dressing-gown. 'Rats is in the kitchen.'

'Quick!' Robbie said. 'She's gone mad, I expect, like in – like in something where someone goes mad. She sleepwalks, see, and she doesn't know what she's doing –'

'Oh, I expect she does.'

'– she does it all the time, see, you don't know what she's like. One time she even got up and turned all the taps on, and Dad said, "Good job it wasn't the gas" and the *next* time she did it, she –'

'Robbie, can you stop panicking?'

'I can if you come and see her.'

Back in Emma's bedroom, the bug-eyed excluder waited. Emma opened her eyes suddenly and met its gaze full-on. Suddenly she felt a bit sorry for it. It was no picnic, being an excluder. People kicked and trampled you. They didn't bother to ask. A rumble in the hall. A door slamming. Someone was coming – *listen* –

Big feet down the hall. Big feet over the excluder. Big feet stopping in horror.

'Emma!' Gran Dodd's jaw dropped. 'Emma! *What have you done?*'

'What?' Emma Gifford struggled upright in bed. 'Nothing, I don't think – have I?'

'Bad news, Emma, you've gone mad,' Robbie told her.

'I'm afraid something's happened in the bathroom,' Gran Dodd said. 'The chair in the bath's fallen over, and there's blackberry juice –'

'All over the bedroom? All over the bedroom carpet? All – all over *me*?' Emma looked down at herself. 'It's me again, isn't it?' Emma said. 'What have I been *doing*?'

She looked around in horror. The door-snake smiled its smile, deeply purple in places, like the carpet, the door, the duvet, the bedside light she'd knocked over and anything else she'd touched, like her nightie – like Emma Gifford.

'Nightmare *City*,' Robbie said. 'It looked really bad when I came in. I thought –'

'What?' Emma recovered some attitude. 'I'd murdered Rats or something?'

'Where *is* Rats?'

'In the kitchen.'

'Was he indoors last night? I mean, upstairs at all – in my bedroom?'

The Excluder

'Forget Rats. You got up in the night, remember? You must've sleepwalked in the bathroom and done something stupid.'

'*You* never noticed.'

'I never put the light on.'

'Even so.'

'Well, excuse *me* if I don't check someone's not got in the bath and tipped up the basin.'

It wasn't even *her* fault. That was the hard part about it. The excluder's crummy-looking smile finally got to Emma Gifford. She jumped up and threw it downstairs.

'I'm sorry, Gran, I don't like it. I never did.'

'Well, it's been a funny night. But never mind that now,' Gran Dodd got up. It was nothing a nice cup of tea wouldn't fix. 'I'm going downstairs to put the kettle on.'

'But, Gran, your carpet – it'll stain –' Emma swallowed. 'It wasn't even my fault. It was the excluder that did it.'

'Yeah, right,' Robbie said. 'Stuffed Snake Goes Mad In Bathroom.'

'I mean, it was *because* of the excluder – it scared me, Gran. I fell asleep and when I woke up *it had moved* –'

'It'd *moved*?' Robbie widened his eyes. 'Did it leave an *address*?'

'– and I woke up and it was *watching* me, and it was like it wanted to keep me out of the rest of the house so I couldn't get help. But I got out anyway and then I went in the bathroom—'

'– and got in the bath,' Robbie finished. 'Like you do, in the middle of the night.'

'*Fell* in the bath, actually. I've got bruises, see?'

Robbie saw. So did Gran Dodd. 'I think –' said Gran Dodd, '– I think I may have –' said Gran Dodd. 'I think it's all my fault.'

'What d'you mean?' Emma asked.

'The thing is, I looked in on you last night before I went to bed, and it never occurred to me that you might not *like* it under your door, and of course I might have –'

'You looked in?' Emma stared. 'I didn't see you looking in.'

'You were fast asleep, so I –'

'So you closed the door again and went away *And the door opening moved the snake.*'

Of course, the snake had been pushed by the door. How else would it have moved? Emma felt the mood

of the night draining away with relief. It seemed like
a nightmare now, mainly because it was. Imagining a
draught excluder could get her somehow. Or exclude
her from anything in the house. It was pretty wild. So
wild, she needed time in a long, hot shower to backtrack
over everything she'd said, hopefully nothing *too* cringe-
making. Nothing had happened except that she'd
sleepwalked somehow and got tangled up in the bathroom
with the blackberry-jelly-juice stuff. She couldn't think
how she'd done it. Of course, she'd sleepwalked before.
But never into the *bath*. It must be staying at Gran's.
That was it. Staying at Gran's made you mad.

'We'll throw that snake away now, shall we?' Gran
Dodd said, over breakfast. 'It's caused enough trouble
for one night.'

'It's not *it's* fault, it's mine.'

'We'll get one of those cats,' Gran said firmly, 'one of
those nice cats with the long tails that stop the draught.
I've seen them in the market. They've got them in purple
or orange – which d'you think you'd like?'

Poor old door-snake. After breakfast, Emma rescued
it from the stair-well and considered its stains. Rats
watched her solemnly from a kitchen chair. The smell
of hot blackberries filled the house. Amazingly, Emma

hadn't upset the basin of juice in the bath, only washed her hands in it somehow. It was nothing a *rolling boil* wouldn't fix. There would be plenty of blackberry juice, after all, to make the jelly, plus the stains in the carpet weren't disastrous, being as the carpet was purple. No one could have dreamt the night's happenings would turn out OK – not even Gnid Blyton – but they did. Except for the mess, it was funny. Robbie wasn't about to let her forget it.

'Bonkers, or what?' he insisted. 'Mrs Mad of Mad Street. Yes,' he went on in a stupid voice, 'yes I *do* tend to get up in the night and take a bath in blackberry juice. I find it quite cold this time of year, but I *do* like a purple bum –'

Emma let it bounce off her. Except for the stained old excluder, excluded for ever from the possibility of looking trim under any door ever again, with his purple blackberry blotches and his crushed and knowing smile, no one would have known Emma Gifford had excluded anything at all from her morning, not even sorting Robbie.

Planet Biro

Just *thinking* about Luke Stuart's *Beach Party Summer Mix* CD made Becky Stott so mad she felt like smashing it when she found it. *If* she ever found it. Becky Stott hated losing things. She'd lost things before, plenty of things, but the *Beach Party* CD really got to her. Borrowed from Lisa Stuart's brother, it wasn't about to go away – except that it already *had*, and that was the problem. So she'd had Luke Stuart's CD two, almost three months, so far – she'd find it, wouldn't she, in the end? Lisa Stuart wasn't convinced. Lisa Stuart had been *really stressy* about it twice already this week. Lisa Stuart wasn't *ever* going to let her forget about it, even if Luke Stuart did.

Fever Dreams

She searched her room. She searched the car. She searched the bins outside. Finally Becky Stott lay awake at night in a blaze of concentration. *Where the stuff had it got to?* She closed her eyes tight and imagined hard, as hard as any mind-reader in any magic act, harder, even, than Mystic Meg searching her mystic ball. With enormous effort, Becky Stott imagined the *Beach Party Summer Mix* blazing a flaming trail across her mind, drawing her, irresistibly, to the place where it had irritatingly lain hidden so long, despite her best effort to find it. First it drew her under the bed. Then to the gap behind the bookcase. Then the blazing trail pulsed vaguely behind the wardrobe. Finally it faded and died, mainly because she was imagining it. She tried coming in from outer space, zeroing in on Earth, then Europe, then England, Sussex, Townley and Worthal by degrees, homing in on Durland Close, number nineteen, then *inside* number nineteen, then the living room of number nineteen, then the dusty bracket behind the shelving units in the living room of number nineteen, where *somewhere* she'd see a CD – but it was no good. No way was the *Beach Party Summer Mix* going to light up and sing till she found it. No way would it draw her to it. She would have to find it the hard way.

Planet Biro

Sweeping her eyes round her bedroom, Becky Stott felt hopeless. Hadn't she searched it twice already and come up with a giant headache and not a lot else, not counting the glitter pen she'd thrown at Claire Blatchford *years* ago and found behind the bookcase covered in fluff? What was the point in starting again? Pulling everything out all over the floor and getting all hot and cross? Stuffing it all away again, much worse, after you'd trodden on something and broken it? How had she come to have so much *stuff* in her room to look through in the *first* place, most of it rubbish, including those stupid trolls? The trolls standing in a row on the top of Becky Stott's computer were less than no help at all, with their ever-open arms and their shocks of candy-floss hair and their fixed smiles, which always looked nasty after a while, the more you stared. Where to begin? Where – or how – to ever end? Becky Stott sighed. She might have known a bedroom thick with soft toys, joss sticks, incense oils, linen flowers, moisturisers, candles, feathers, ethnic pots and a million little bottles would be less than likely to give up a lost CD without a struggle. But still. It had to be *somewhere*.

It would be good if she could just go to sleep and forget about it now, except – Becky Stott sat up.

Fever Dreams

Leaping out of bed on a sudden inspiration, she rushed downstairs to the shoe cupboard and tore out the hats and the blankets, the squash rackets, shoe-cleaning kit, aluminium chairs and the stack of board games underneath. She fought quite a while with the aluminium chairs and the bags of Christmas balls and lights in the darkness under the stairs. She had to drag out *every single thing* in the end. In the end she had to put it all back again. Of course Luke Stuart's *Beach Party* CD wouldn't be under the stairs in the shoe cupboard. It was getting silly, now.

With a growing sense of despair, Becky Stott stumped back upstairs. The stupid thing was, the stupid *Beach Party* CD was probably less than three metres from anywhere she stood at *any given point in the stupid pigging house*, if only she knew how to *see* it. She could picture herself playing it in the living room, snapping it back into its cheesy case and thinking, *Mustn't lose this* – then, right after that, she lost it. It wasn't fair. Why couldn't someone make a fluorescent thingy you marked things with, so they glowed when you couldn't find 'em? If they could make smart cat-flaps and virtual pubs on the internet, it wasn't *too* much to ask.

Once upstairs, Becky Stott cast around an eye terrible

with irritation and the kind of determination that might actually tackle the – whisper it – *cupboard on the landing*. Except it wouldn't be there. The nightmare cupboard on the landing was one step beyond any meaningful search. Luke Stuart's CD had no reason to be in it, so nothing but utter hopelessness could make anyone suffer inside it, and nothing but direful consequences could possibly ensue, once the landing cupboard, untouched since the last desperate search for something *else* impossible, was once, irresistibly, stirred up. But it *had* to be in the house somewhere, and she – Becky Stott – was going to find it, if she had to stay up all night. Or whatever. Yawning so wide she heard her jaw click, Becky Stott sat on her bed.

Why didn't she simply replace it? Apart from the fact that she didn't want to, it would take up all her Saturday wages from her morning cleaning job down the road, money she had earmarked for something more gorgeous than a boring replacement CD. Becky Stott climbed crossly back into bed. She wouldn't replace it, she would *find* it. Why couldn't it bleep? Let her know its location by psychic means or something? Closing her eyes again, sleepy by now, Becky Stott grew heavy-limbed in bed. She felt a bit psychic tonight. She wouldn't force it, this time. She would relax and let it come to her. It couldn't be too long in coming. She would *feel* where the *Beach Party* had gone . . .

Next morning, Becky Stott had cookery, plus art, plus a netball match after school. She crossly got her ingredients out of the fridge and jammed them into a tin. Crossly, she packed her trainers and shirt. Then she remembered her art.

Pounding furiously up the stairs, she finally found a hairbrush. After she'd wound her hair into a bun so tight it gave her a headache, she searched around for her homework. Twenty past eight already. She'd put it down on the floor last night. Where could it have *got* to?

'Twenty-five past eight,' Mrs Stott shouted, helpfully. 'Aren't you running late?'

'I can't find my art folder *anywhere*.' Becky Stott appeared tragically at the top of the stairs.

'I thought you were doing art homework last night.'

'I was, but now it's gone. What am I going to *do*?'

Mrs Stott took a chance. 'Keep a tidier room?'

Becky Stott disappeared on an impulse. The sounds of last-minute searching and the slap of books overturned added extra drama to the whingeing that drifted downstairs. 'Of course, it *couldn't* be where I left it – that'd be *too* easy –'

'Becky!'

'WHAT?'

'You've probably missed the bus. I'll run you into school if you like.'

'Stupid books – so *fall* on the floor. Wonderful. Just great.'

'What's going on up there?' Mrs Stott tried again. 'Becky, it's time to go.'

'Mum, what's *wrong* with me?' Becky Stott clumped slowly downstairs. 'Why does *everything* I put down somewhere just *vanish*?'

'I think *somewhere's* the key word in there.'

'But where does everything lost *go* to? It must go *somewhere*, all together. I bet all together somewhere there's huge great *wodges* of stuff people've lost, stuff like –'

'Have you got your trainers?'

' – keys and contact lenses and the things people put on the tops of their cars and then drive away without, and umbrellas and teddy-bears and stuff like that, and *one red wellington* and old people's sticks and glasses and, like, *one* earring or something, and millions and millions of biros –'

'How about your cookery stuff?'

'Got it. I bet if you added up *all the biros anyone ever lost*, there's *zillions* gone missing somewhere. Probably there's a *planet* Biro, or something – and what I want to know is –'

'*And* your project folder?'

'– and what I want to know is, who's got 'em?' Becky Stott drew breath. 'My project folder? Um. No. I haven't.'

Later that day, after maths with Mr Smedley, Lisa Stuart was more insistent than ever. She was really teeing Becky off, but Becky bore it anyway.

'So, when?' Lisa Stuart struck a pose like she'd waited for ever.

'When, what?'

'When are you bringing in my brother's CD?'

'I'm looking for it, all right?'

'So look harder.'

'I *am* looking – what d'you want me to say?'

Lisa Stuart considered. 'How about, "I'll replace it, I'll bring in the money tomorrow"?'

'No need,' Becky Stott smiled sweetly. 'I'll find it, OK? Tonight.'

Planet Biro

'If you can't, bring in the money.'

'I told you. I'll find it tonight.'

After the home game that night (a loss, 4–2, to Longham Comp), Becky Stott flung down her netball strip in the hall and took a long and well-earned shower. If only she could wash Lisa Stuart out of her hair as easily as the days aggravations. Visions of the lurid, swirling cover design of the *Beach Party* CD had haunted her, on and off, all day. It was somewhere close, she knew it. Somewhere close, but stupid.

After tea and telly and a whole bunch of congruent triangles for Mr Smedley, Becky Stott sat dimly over her computer. A half-finished essay on Erosion Values at Holderness blinked away in front of her, instantly replaced by a wraparound screen-saver announcing: *Rebecca Stott's PC. Hands Off . . .*

The trolls on the top of the computer watched Becky Stott do her homework. She did it pretty quickly, usually, any time after *EastEnders*. But tonight she was tired and cross. She did the assignment anyhow but all the time she was doing it, the trolls looked down and grinned. On an impulse, she pushed them over, but it didn't seem to help. The Factors enabling Shingle Shift swam in front of her eyes. The trolls were telling her something.

Even their feet were annoying. She stood them up and carried on. The feeling grew stronger and stronger.

She looked up suddenly. '*What?*'

The trolls clustered mutely and stared. What if they came alive? If they ever did, they'd be nasty, Becky felt convinced. And if they spoke at all, it would be in micey little voices like budgies pecking you death.

Now and again, someone had the right idea. In a perfect world, it wouldn't happen. But the statistical chances of someone, some time, hitting the nail on the head were about two million to one in any generation, and this time around, Becky Stott was *it*. She was right about Planet Biro. Right about the trolls. Planet Biro was real, and the trolls on the computer were evil. True. It was just as simple as that.

The fact was, Planet Biro was a reality. So was Planet String and Planet Rubber Band. So was Planet Art Homework, Planet Lost Sock and Planet Kitchen Scissors, not to mention Planet Petrol Cap and, of course, Planet CD. Every lost thing had a place, and there was a place for every lost thing. Somewhere no one could find it . . .

Planet Biro

The trolls looked down at Becky Stott doing her homework from the top of the computer and they suddenly knew that she knew. It was all the same to the trolls – six trolls – whether Becky Stott got an A grade or no grade at all for Erosion at Holderness, so long as she didn't look up too often the way she just did, with the question written large in her eyes. Where had Luke Stuart's CD *really* gravitated to? Plus everything else, ever, she'd lost in a *lifetime* of losing things.

The answer was terribly simple. The right explanations usually are. The fact was, the improbable truth was, the trolls *actually took things and hid them.*

Becky Stott looked up a time or two more. The trolls kept it straight, like they had to. Distantly related to crabbed old story-book sprites like Rumpelstiltskin and the elves that cobbled shoes for the Brothers Grimm, cousins in the seventh degree to the Elves of Spring in the *Rupert* books with all their underground engines, they'd kept a straight face since the sixties, when plastic trolls had first appeared – from Denmark, it was rumoured. Inhabiting their plastic bodies for mischief throughout the night had been easy, at first, until other fads had taken over. Fluffy nylon Gonks with hard plastic feet had proved a bit of a lean period for any sprites needing neat plastic bodies for midnight adventures, with Barbie and My Little Pony.

But Trolls had come back with a vengeance. Other things had come back in between. Now Troffles, third generation Trolls, had reappeared in cereal packets, and gaily topped pencils everywhere. They lined the top of Becky Stott's computer, with their ever-open arms, their slightly sinister smiles and their brushes of baby-blue – and green and yellow and pink – hair, and they never said a thing. Little did anyone know they jumped around at night, squeaking madly – Becky Stott was right about the voices – squeaking madly and moving everything around, for *no other reason than to annoy*, because that was the way they were made.

Becky Stott slept uneasily that night. She hadn't found the *Beach Party* CD. She hadn't finished Erosion at Holderness. Something – what? – was bothering her. Tomorrow she'd dump the trolls. She was sick of seeing them on top of the computer. They'd only been put there for a joke. Maybe she'd post them to Lisa Stuart.

Maybe they'd bring her bad luck . . .

While Becky Stott slept uneasily, the six trolls lifted her biros. Magnetically and irresistibly, from pocket, pencilcase and school bag, they drifted off to join Planet

Planet Biro

Biro – composed, already, of every lost biro in history. It existed in almost every place, but could be summoned outside a bedroom window after midnight with very little trouble. The six trolls summoned it speedily. Planet Biro revolved, glistening and clicking very slightly as a zillion retractables clicked on and off till they broke, right outside number nineteen Durland Close. Then it spun grandly away. The six trolls twittered and burped and moved things around until morning. Then they danced on the duvet and pulled Becky Stott's hair and nails. They existed just to annoy. No one said they were nice.

Next day, Lisa Stuart wheeled out the heavy artillery
'Let me guess. You haven't got it.'
'I'm still looking, OK?'
'And you didn't bring in the money.'
'Right first time. So?'
'So my brother'll see you after school.'
'Oh, no. I'm scared.'
'You owe me the price of a CD.'
'I owe *Luke* the price of a CD.'
'He told me to ask you, all right? Bring it in tomorrow.'
'You don't have to tell me. I *know*.'

Fever Dreams

Becky Stott had trouble finding anything to write with all that day, but she thought no more about Planet Biro until eight fifteen the next evening when she sat down to do her homework.

'Where's all my biros gone?' she asked the inside of her pencilcase. 'I had a green one and a red one. Mum! Plus my multi-colour. *Mum!*'

'What?'

'Did you take all my biros and not put them back?'

'Why would I?' Mrs Stott said, crossly. 'I thought you'd taken mine. The biros I bought the other day at the newsagent seem to have vanished. I don't know where they've all got to – I couldn't even sign a cheque for petrol this morning, the filling station didn't have any, either.'

Nothing further was said until Mr Stott became *very annoyed indeed* when no pen could be found beside the phone when his sailing mate Jimmy Grigson rang, and he – Dave Stott – came to write down racing times and fixtures, except that he couldn't, seeing as there was nothing to write with.

'Where's all the biros?' he roared. *'There's never any biros in this house!'*

Which wasn't quite true, as Becky Stott pointed out.

But she *did* start to wonder what had happened, next morning, when the postman turned up with a parcel and no pen anywhere in sight.

'Recorded delivery. Can you sign for this parcel?' The postman patted his pockets.

'I would, if I had something to sign with.' Becky Stott said, yawning.

'Can't help you there.' the postman said. 'There's no flipping biros at the depot.'

The situation was dire in school. It even got to Lisa Stuart.

'Becks, lend us a biro, will you?' she said at registration.

Becky Stott smiled sweetly. 'Sorry,' she said, 'I wouldn't lend you a biro if you were signing a contract with Hollywood. Plus, I haven't got one.'

Everyone went biro-less that day and most of the next, and nothing much got written down at all and no one found out what had happened, until a broadcast from the surface of Planet Biro hit Becky Stott in the left ear at precisely 8.46 p.m. the day after *that*, a Thursday, right after she put down the phone and said, 'No luck at Sarah's.'

'What?' Mr Stott looked up.

'Sarah hasn't got *it*.'

'What?'

'Luke Stuart's stupid CD. Oh, can you hear? What was *that*?'

'What?' Mr Stott asked, for the third time.

'*Weird*.' Becky Stott cupped her ear. 'I'm hearing something, voices it sounds like – *We've got your CD*.'

Mr Stott folded his paper. 'Becks, will you sit down?'

'They're laughing at me – at *all* of us.' Still listening, Becky sat down. Then she said, 'They sound really strange, Dad – like mice.'

'You don't want to get so worked up,' Mr Stott said, carefully. 'Is school-work getting you down? I'll lend you a bit, if you like, towards replacing your friend's whatever-it-is, if it worries you that much.'

'Dad,' Becky said, 'you don't have to.'

'It's not surprising things go missing in this madhouse. I've yet to find a biro beside the phone, and as for a bit of string or the back-door *key* when you want it,' Mr Stott paused. Words failed him. 'I'd give an arm and a leg,' he went on bitterly, 'to find out where my electric shaver went to. I haven't seen it *once* since the Association dinner in Cardiff.'

Planet Biro

'Dad, they *take things and hide them* – really!' Becky was actually laughing. 'They took Luke Stuart's CD. Don't bother lending me money. I know how to get it back now.'

That night, well after midnight, Becky Stott put a final full-stop to Erosion at Holderness. She'd left it late deliberately. So much less time to wait. At exactly twenty-six minutes past midnight, she threw open her bedroom window and lined up six trolls along the sill. She didn't have to ask them, or make any threats. She didn't have to plead or beg or bribe. The game was up, and they knew it.

'*Go on, then.*' she whispered. '*Get on with it.*'

In time-honoured fashion, she looked away at the vital moment. Nobody ever saw Rumpelstiltskin spinning gold out of straw, did they? Nobody ever – did they? – sat up and watched the little elves cobbling shoes in the night, not in any fairytale, ever. How many people saw magic things and didn't – guaranteed – go mad?

All the same, she listened. Would she ever forget the silvery sound as Planet CD docked outside? The rainbow lights that played on the wall as it nudged the open window? The breathless moment it hung there, shedding compact discs like scales, among them *Beach Party*?

Would she ever forget the clicking of Planet Biro – had she heard it some time before? – the clicking of Planet Biro, as it interrupted its grand revolution to scatter busy ball-points thickly over the floor? The buzzing of Planet Shaver as Dad's long-lost Philishave homed in on his bedside table like some demented pigeon?

Next day, Becky Stott slapped Luke Stuart's *Beach Party Summer Mix* CD straight into his hand after school.

He looked up vaguely. 'Thanks. Didn't know you had it.'

'You mean, you didn't tell Lisa to give me a hard time about it?'

'Sorry?'

'You didn't ask me for money?'

'I will, if you want me to.'

'Your sister,' Becky Stott made a face. 'Your sister, you know she's a pain?'

Luke was really quite nice. 'Tell me about it,' he said.

Queen of the Smooth

I'm not supposed to tell about you this but it looks like I'm going to anyway, except I don't know how much I told you already when I wrote things when I was younger. Did I tell you I had this thing about Queen of the Smooth? Queen of the Smooth was this *feeling* I used to get when I was little, especially if I was hot, especially if I had headaches. I still get Queen of the Smooth, except now I know what she means. I used to get bugbears, too. I think I told you about the bugbears. That time when they said I had flu, and I thought I had bears in my wardrobe?

It wasn't flu at all. I didn't know it at the time, but that was my first migraine. That was the reason I felt sick. They didn't call it migraine, at first. At first they called it Cyclical Sickness with Recurrent Stress-related Headaches. *Now* they call it migraine. They say emotional factors can trigger an attack. That means it's all in my mind. Try telling that to someone else who has migraine. See what they have to say next.

I've got over bugbears now, a long time ago, in fact. Now I'm fourteen, I've got Aidan's old room. It's the same room I had when I thought there were bears in the wardrobe. I used to get upset after that. That's why Aidan had it. Then Mum moved out, and Dad moved into *my* room and made *me* move back into Aidan's after *Aidan* moved out. The room's OK, I suppose, except I asked Dad to move the wardrobe three times – but it makes me think about Aidan.

My brother Aidan went off to college last year. I miss him loads, but I'm not about to tell *him* that. Sometimes he e-mails me jokes, then usually I e-mail some back. It helps, but it's not the same. Aidan likes being at college. He's studying to teach PE. He doesn't come home that often. I think he thinks home's pretty dull. It is, except how would *I* know? Except for Dad I'm on my own now, but I don't get scared on my own any more, even after I'm ill. I'm ill quite often these days, so the Queen of the Smooth comes a lot. Once she comes to smooth away the lights and patterns – the patterns make me feel sick – I know my migraine's going at last, so at least I know someone *cares*. I'm sorry, but to me she's real. At least, she's *real important*. She would be to you, if you knew what my headaches were like. Did I mention migraine's no fun?

'Are you all right?' Dad usually shouts.

Dad's no help at all. He doesn't know what to do. Usually when he shouts, I hear it like sick yellow whorls.

'Yes, I'm OK – just tired,' I usually manage to say, except when I'm feeling that sick I don't say anything at all.

Queen of the Smooth usually fixes it. I know when she's coming, by the way the patterns change. The patterns make me feel terrible. They've got a horrible atmosphere, like everything's brown, and bursting up in prickly shapes, and nothing makes sense any more, and it never made sense to *start* with. Normally I get flashes of light to start with. Then I get crisscross lines, usually red and yellow, usually a horrible grid with layers and layers all *turning* and stuff, and each layer's worse than the one before and the lines get more and more complicated, so no matter *how* hard I shut my eyes they only get worse, until finally I get this sick yellow light and then it's Queen of the Smooth. As soon as she comes the mood changes and everything goes calm and flat and shiny and after a while I go to sleep, and when I wake up I can get up at last and at last the migraine's over. That's how it usually is. But, lately, something's changed.

'No need to mention it at school,' Dad told me the other morning.

'Mention what at school?'

'You know. Queen of the Smooth.'

'I'm not about to, am I?'

'I'm only suggesting you don't. It's only a dream when you're ill.'

'So?'

'You've been talking in your sleep. Is there something on your mind?'

Oh, no, I felt like saying, everything in the garden's rosy. You and Mum split up. *You* act like a bear with a sore head. I don't have Aidan, either. What *should* be on my mind?

'Well?'

'Nothing more than usual,' I mumbled.

Queen of the Smooth

'So put a sock in Queen of the Smooth?'

'I *know*. You don't have to tell me.'

It's only a dream when you're ill. So put a sock in it.
Dad was wrong. She was more than that.

Queen of the Smooth was someone I could *rely* on. I
knew she would always come when I needed her most,
spreading her *feeling* around her, like a cool, silky robe
or a cloak. She and I both know I couldn't make it
without her. She never let me down yet. Unlike Dad,
I have to say.

'I'm going round to Mum's after school,' I told Dad.
'Dad, did you hear what I said?'

Dad smiled, the way he smiles when he isn't really
listening. 'Go ahead. I'm playing squash. I'll see you
after eight.'

'After Eight,' I joked. 'Bring a box back, why don't
you?'

But I don't think he heard me over the news. Time
was, Mum would've said something. There was a time,
Mum would've said: 'Can't you give Adam some
attention? Do you have to hear *every* bit of news?' Now
she doesn't need to, seeing as she's living down the road.
There was a time, not so long ago, when she and Dad
argued every minute. Now they're living apart they can't

even argue any more, unless they shout down the road at each another. They used to do that, as well.

After school had finished up and the bus bell had rung and rung, after I'd stayed back catching up on coursework, as usual – I have to catch up all the time, I'm away from school such a lot – I took a sackful of homework round to Mum's. Mum said the same thing as Dad: 'Feeling OK? You look peaky.'

They're always saying things like that. Sometimes I don't even answer.

'Everything all right at home?'

'Fine.' I nodded loads. What did she think I was going to say? Medical science tells me I'll never have another headache? I *like* you living down the road?

'Aidan's home on the ninth,' Mum said. 'He rang me from college last night.'

'Is he?' I said. 'That's great.'

'Yes, and he's got his girlfriend – Amy, I think he said – catching the same train as he is, only *she* gets off at Gloucester and he's coming on without her, but he might go back up and see her, I think he said the sixteenth – hope he doesn't, don't you? It isn't much time at home, but then, he'll do what he likes. They're catching the nine-forty train. He's bringing lots of stuff home, but

first he has to sign out, and so does Anna – Amy – and
he's leaving his first-year texts behind, he's got *millions*
of things to carry –'

'Hope he brings me some goodies.' Millions of things
to carry. It sounded promising.

Mum went on about Aidan – she hadn't even heard
what I said. Whenever Aidan's mentioned, Mum kind
of lights up inside. My brother Aidan's a head-case. He
brings *loads* of things home when he comes – hats,
scarves, badges, stickers, boots, gloves, football strip, all
the gear – things he gets through college, so much he
can hardly carry it, usually all for me. 'PE student's
perks,' he says. 'Helps that I run the college shop.'

Usually Aidan gets lots of stuff cheap, then worries
about carrying it afterwards. He can hardly lift his cases
sometimes so Dad has to fetch him in the car. Sometimes
he and Dad argue all the way home, but Aidan says,
'Not to worry.' Aidan never worries. I like it when
Aidan's home. I hardly ever feel ill.

'I'm sure Aidan's got something for you,' Mum said.
'He hasn't forgotten you yet.' She got up and put on the
kettle. Then she said the same thing as Dad: 'You won't
go on about Queen of the Smooth? When Aidan's home,
I mean.'

'That's what Dad said. Why would I?'

'You're looking pale,' Mum said. 'You could do with some time with Aidan.' Then she thought of something. 'Remember when you were frightened of bears in your wardrobe? When you had Aidan's old room?'

'I wasn't frightened.'

'You were.'

'Anyway,' I said, 'he can have it back, if he wants. Dad made me switch rooms again, and I don't even *like* Aidan's room.'

'Dad put you back in Aidan's room? Why?'

'Wanted more light for his computer.' I shrugged. 'I don't know why he did it.'

'But you used to have nightmares in that room.'

'At least he's moving the wardrobe. When he gets round to it.'

Five days later, Aidan came home. He came home in college colours, mainly maroon and green – the colour of the scarf he gave me. That might we went out to Kingburger with Dad. Dad had Chick Fritters and Baked Potato, Aidan and me had Chilli Dogs with King Fries. I ate until I was stuffed, and so did Aidan.

I pushed back my chair and said, 'That's it, I'm stuffed.'

'How refined,' Dad said.

How refined. He said it in a funny way. He had that nasty look. Dad's pretty sarcastic, at times. Particularly with waitresses. The waitress showed up now 'Everything all right for you, sir?'

Dad looked round like a basking shark. 'Fine, if you *like* a baked potato cooked three days ago and warmed up.'

'Dad,' I said, '*please.*'

'I'm sorry, sir? Is something not to your liking?'

'You could say that. See this?' Dad forked up his baked potato. It didn't look too great. About as great as I felt. 'How many times have you microwaved this potato?'

'All our potatoes were freshly cooked this morning,' the waitress said, although they weren't. She had white hair with very black roots, and she hated people like Dad. *I* hated people like Dad. 'Would you like another potato, sir?'

'Why would I?' Dad said. 'One's enough.'

I could've died, and so could Aidan. Dad didn't feel he'd been out unless he'd made a scene about *something*. We got him talking rugby while the waitress cleared away. We were on pretty safe ground with rugby. Aidan plays rugby at college. He plays all kinds of sports. He has a lot of fun. I can't wait to go to college. Except I'm not fit like Aidan so I probably won't even go.

The waitress brought us dessert. She never even looked at Dad. Dad was more or less OK all through the Mississippi Mud Pie and the Banana Boat Treats me and Aidan had ordered. Dad drank his coffee and glared over his cup at the table in the window having a party. They had paper hats and party poppers and a triple-layer birthday cake and singing waiters and a whole bunch of glitter balloons. Everyone stamped and shouted. They were having a really good time.

'Fuss about nothing,' Dad said. 'I wish I had my paper.'

'I wish you had it, too,' Aidan said, kind of sharply.

Aidan talked more about college. That was OK for a while. He asked me how school was going, but I didn't want to talk about that. Finally we ran out of things to say, so we sat and drank Slush Kups in silence while Dad finished up his coffee.

'Coming round Welchie's?' Aidan asked. 'That's where I'm going after.'

'When?' I said.

'Now,' Aidan winked. 'To get out, you know, to get some fresh air in the park.'

'Oh,' I said, 'right,' I said, 'yeah.'

We both got up too quickly.

'Hello, are we going now?' Dad got up, as well.

'I'm taking Adam to Welchie's,' Aidan said smoothly. 'We won't be back very late.'

'Roland Welch's, you mean?'

'Thanks a million for dinner. See you later, Dad.'

We didn't go round to Welchie's at all. Roland Welch was – had been – a good mate of Aidan's at school. They'd played on the school team together. But now Roland Welch had gone away, probably working as a mechanic, probably somewhere near London. He always liked messing around under a car, did Roland Welch. I can only ever remember him covered in oil. But that night after we left Dad at Kingburger, me and Aidan didn't go round Welchie's house at all like we said we would, because Welchie wouldn't be there. Instead, we sat in the park. It was the same park I'd had my bugbears thing about, when I was little. That time I thought there were bears in the bins, and they bugged me all the way home?

The bridge over the cacky duckpond and the swings and the benches and the sheds – and even the kiddies playground – were in just the same places, of course, only older now and more chopped around and smellier. The bins by the swings, where I used to think the bears rooted around for rubbish so they could keep fat and healthy, just right for following me home, were just the same old bins by the same old swings they'd always been, and the park was the same old park, except that Aidan didn't play there on a Saturday morning any more.

'Get much time for footie?' I asked Aidan, after a while.

Aidan was miles away. 'Sorry, Codge, what did you say?'

He used to call me Codge when I was little, I don't know why. There never was a reason. It sounded funny, now. Aidan thought so, too.

'Sorry, it just slipped out.'

'I don't mind,' I said. 'Really.' I really didn't mind.

'Adam,' he said, 'remember when Mum lived at home? Remember Saturdays, we'd watch Saturday morning telly and then go up the park? And sometimes there'd be a match on and sometimes a you'd watch or Dad would –'

'D'you play much at college?' I said. 'I mean football, not rugby or anything.'

'I told you I did. What's the matter?'

Queen of the Smooth

'I forgot, I suppose. I don't remember *everything* you tell me.'

Aidan got up and kicked a can around.

'Aren't you in my room, now?'

'Yeah.'

'With the bugbears?'

'Yeah.' Aidan remembered. I grinned.

'No bears in your wardrobe now, then?'

'No, but there's Queen of the Smooth. She comes when I have my headaches.'

Aidan looked at me seriously. 'You should get out more.'

'Don't you ever get bored at college?' I asked him, after a moment.

'Bored with having a great time?' Aidan laughed. He had a big laugh. 'Sorry, no, I don't.'

'Is it really that good, then?' I must've sounded dopey. 'Don't you ever wish you were at home?'

'Not really, there's too much to do, plus we go out most nights. There's some really good pubs down the road. Amy likes the Feathers, but usually we go to the Mitre, then sometimes we go to the Boar – then there's work, of course. Amy does loads of work, I'm always going, "Amy! *No!* Come out with me instead!" Most people say they don't *do* any work, but that's just what they *say* – I'm doing judo, did you know?'

'No,' I said. 'I didn't know. Does *Amy* do judo, too?'

'Amy plays hockey.'

'Nice for some.'

Aidan looked at me. 'You'll get away some time, don't worry.'

I shrugged. 'I know I will.'

We got up and walked back the long way, past our old primary school. We didn't want to remember it much. Just the smell was enough. When we got to the top of our road, Aidan stopped. Aidan was staying with Mum. I'd be going back to our place alone.

Aidan looked at me. 'How are you, really?' he said.

There were millions of things I could've said, but in the end I said nothing. Probably Mum was watching already, behind the nets at number eight. Probably I should be going. Probably I had homework to do. I did. I did have homework.

'I miss you, you know,' Aidan said.

I didn't say anything.

'This won't last for ever,' Aidan said.

'No,' I said, 'it won't last for ever. I'll miss you too, when you're gone.'

Queen of the Smooth

Finally Aidan put on his stupid face. Then he did his Hunchback along Mum's wall. After he'd finally made me laugh, Aidan said, 'Bye for now' Then he said the one thing that might've cheered me up. Aidan grinned and duffed me once in the arm. Then he said: 'Coming up Hog Fair tomorrow?'

Hog Fair's this really big deal. It's this huge great fair that comes every year in the night – it doesn't, but that's how it seems – and when you wake up it's just *there*. It's like, you go down the Square and you can't even recognize places you've known all your life because everything looks so different. Hog Fair takes over the whole town with stalls and rides and hot-dog booths and shies and Shove Penny arcades and snaking cables and caravans and people selling bulbs and tights and china and vegetable peelers and paint rollers and everything else you can think of. It's cheap and it's chatty and kind of old-fashioned, but everyone goes. It's a buzz. I used to go with Aidan every year. One year we went on *everything* and we'd had spaghetti for tea, and we made ourselves really sick, so Aidan threw up on the bus. This year, I wasn't going to go. Not till Aidan asked me.

Fever Dreams

Me and Dad went out about eight o'clock. The lights of the fair were crazy. They lit up the whole town. I could feel they were drawing us down to them, same as they did every year. Every year, the same smell of boiling onions. Every year, the big wheel going round. This time last year Aidan had just gone to college. First year I ever missed Hog Fair.

I met Aidan by the dodgems and we sussed out the rides right away. This year's hot rides were Mega City Rollers and Masterblaster, the only things worth going on. That's what Aidan said. Aidan said, 'Only two rides worth going on. Coming on Masterblaster?'

I nodded a lot. 'Take me to it.'

Dad wandered off in the crowd. Probably he'd watch some salesman scraping paint off a board. *A million uses. Scrape then paint. Doubles as a bottle opener.* Then he'd buy the scraper and put it away and never use it. He always bought something useless, every year.

Aidan and I did the Hog Fair thing for about an hour or two. We'd just got off Masterblaster, when Aidan noticed Judge Dredd. The Judge Dredd ride was cool, but quite expensive. We went on Mega City twice, then Judge Dredd again, then we went on Side Winder, then we – I – ate mallow snakes, then we each had a hot dog, then we ran out of money.

'Let's do the Wheel next,' I said.

'Can't,' Aidan said. 'That's *it*. Unless you've got a secret stash of money.'

Which I hadn't. Which didn't stop me wishing we'd done the Big Wheel. We *always* went on the Big Wheel – how could we have missed it? It wasn't so hot, but it was *there* looking down on the town, every year, always – like so much in my life that wasn't. I *like* things to stay the same. Round and round every year.

Round and round, every year. I watched the Big Wheel while I ate my hot dog, and the fair hummed around us like a machine. It *was* a machine, I thought, a huge great machine that came in the night and sucked up all your money – Round and round on the wheel. *Mum and Dad. Get that.*

'Aidan – Aidan! Look!'

Aidan looked up, and there they were, Mum and Dad, riding the Big Wheel *in the same bucket*, dipping and laughing together. I couldn't take my eyes off them. Every time the Wheel came around it brought me my mum and dad with surprised-looking faces and Mum's hair all over Dad's shoulders – they were even holding on to one another – and they both made me sick, they really did.

Fever Dreams

'They must've bumped into each other.' Aidan grinned – how *could* he? 'Don't often see 'em together.'

Understatement of all time. Suddenly the lights of the fair jumped out at me, the red and the green and the yellow, and they all got complicated somehow, and the patterns whirled and the lights flashed and they were *the same patterns I had in my mind* –

'Adam, don't do this now. Adam – are you all right?'

– and suddenly I knew that I wasn't –
  – and I wanted to let the pain out –
  – a huge pain I'd had for ages –
  – so I did –
  – and Aidan held me till it was over –
  – and then I felt better –
  – and more and more distant –
  – from –
  – the Fading Queen of the Smooth.

Aidan was very angry, I can remember that. We went back to Mum's place that night after the fair, and we all had hot chocolate together, except I felt sick and went to bed. But I heard Aidan telling them off. Aidan told Mum and Dad a lot of things that night that they never knew before. It took him quite a long time. I heard Dad's voice booming a long while after Aidan came up to bed, so I knew he'd stayed on to have a talk with Mum. Probably a talk about me. I didn't care if they talked about me, so long as they were talking.

They talked a lot more after that. Something had changed, I don't know what. When it came time for Aidan to go back to college, we met up and saw him off together. Aidan liked that, I could see.

'Don't worry,' he said to me, 'will you? There's nothing to worry about.'

'No,' I said, 'I won't worry. Can you bring me the new United strip next time?'

Aidan grinned. 'I'll see what I can do.'

'When you're not seeing *Amy*.'

'Don't push it,' said Aidan, 'all right?'

When at last the coach pulled away, I knew I'd seen Aidan for the last time in probably ten weeks, but I felt all right about it this time, which I never usually do. Mum and Dad waved to Aidan. Aidan waved back.Mum and Dad. Together on the tarmac. One wave did them both.

'Well,' Dad said, as Aidan's coach turned the corner,

'one gone, and one to go.'

'The time goes by so quickly,' Mum said, sadly. 'We'll be waving Adam off to college before he knows it.'

I think I *will* know it, though. I felt a lot better after that. I had less time off school because I didn't feel ill so I didn't have so much stuff to catch up so I had time for football on Saturdays – funnily enough, up the park. I even played Aidan's position, but I didn't see any bears. I didn't get so many headaches. I didn't get Queen of the Smooth. The *Fading* Queen of the Smooth.

I think I left her at the fair. I'm glad if I did, I hardly see her these days. I don't really miss her, either. Maybe she went off on holiday with film-star shades and a speedboat, maybe to Acapulco, maybe with the King of the Grid. I don't see him much, either. I hardly ever get grids in my mind, these days, not since Aidan held me that time at Hog Fair, not since I felt so much better.

I don't really need her like I used to. Who knows? Maybe the Fading Queen of the Smooth found someone else who needs her. Maybe she's in someone's wardrobe smoothing out bears or someone else's headache. I don't really care any more. I used to think I held everything – Mum, Dad, Aidan, me, the *world* – in my mind, and wonder if it would all come out right. Some things are too big to carry around inside, and the whole thing with Mum and Dad, it was just too heavy So I put it down, that night after the fair. I put it down just like that. I used to worry too much. I don't worry half so much, now.

Life isn't all a stick of candyfloss. I still feel ill, sometimes. Mum and Dad still argue. Mum's never going to come back and live with us at home. But I know things won't crumble tomorrow. I know that most of the time, most things make sense – which is more than Dad says he knows. He's joking, of course. He jokes a lot more, these days.

'What do you do with a space-man?'

'Search me.'

'Park in it, man.'

Ha ha. That's one of mine, but Dad really likes it. I heard him telling it to Aidan over the phone the other day, except he says 'space-man' all wrong, so you know there's something coming. Still, he tries. He didn't, before. I'm telling you, things've changed. I still get migraines and patterns sometimes. I'll probably always get headaches and patterns sometimes, even when I'm at college or uni like Aidan. But – you know? – I can smooth them out for myself.

Shreddievision

'I got *Dead Reckoning*,' Danny threw down the video on the settee. 'Hope that's OK. There wasn't much else up there. Anyway – it's meant to be scary.'

The others didn't look up.

'Good decision.'

'Weird.'

'*Gross*.'

'Outstanding.'

Reactions were going to be varied. Ali and Zoë were going to want something, well, lighter, with a couple of hot names in it at least. Ben and Jamie Prentice wouldn't care too much. They'd watch pretty well anything.

Shreddievision

Danny peeled off his sweatshirt and threw himself down in a chair. It was nice to be noticed when you got in. Nice to be *appreciated*. He'd only offered to cycle all the way up to Stu Smethick's Video Vaults to get them all the latest releases while the olds went out for their weekly bash at the club. The others had only slobbed around eating tortilla chips all over the floor and actually let him *do* it. No one else had jumped up and offered or done a thing to help out.

'Nice one, Danny,' he thanked himself sarcastically. 'Thanks for cycling your *brains* out. Here's five quid for your trouble. Thanks, don't mind if I do.'

They'd only eaten the Snickers plus all the Extra Hot Chili Chips while he was gone. No one had saved him a thing. You'd think, Danny thought bitterly, you'd think *someone'd –*'

'Move over, can't you?' Ali grumbled. Ali was Danny's sister. Zoë was Danny's sister, too. Ben and Jamie were mates. 'Just come in and take up the whole settee, why don't you?'

'Anyone get me a drink?'

'Plenty of Coke in the kitchen.'

'So no one brings me anything after I went, like, *three miles* up Smethick's and back?'

Ali smiled sweetly. 'I think he's getting the picture.'

Jamie Prentice belched sonorously. 'Especially for you,' he added.

Danny got up and fetched himself a drink.

While he was out in the kitchen he considered making up the traditional Friday night pig-out tray of Hula Hoops, Penguins, choc-chip cookies, etc. Then he stopped himself. No *way* was he about to fetch the Coke and Pringles as *well* as do himself in by going up Smethick's and back. Ali or Zoë could fix up the tray. Then they could put on the movie. Friday night had its rituals. One of them was a top tray of fulsome face-filler – salt and vinegar Chipsticks, pimento-flavour crisps and double-choc Bloaters included. But someone else could get it.

'Anyway,' Danny told the settee, 'someone *else* can get the food. What's left of it, that is.'

'Chill,' Ben said. 'What's the hurry?'

'We're not putting the film on yet, are we?' Zoë got up. She shook out her hair and expertly twisted it up into a tight bun. Then she flicked the table football experimentally.

Ben said, 'Fancy a game?'

Zoë shrugged. 'If you do.'

Shreddievision

Danny lay back and watched the game rage from end to end of what was, by now, a pretty shaky table. The penalty for spinning men or moving the whole table football on its nasty stick-like legs was a throw-in to your opponent, but the table always shifted as the game got more involved and the players more intent on slipping one past the goalie with his plastic legs in the air.

'When did Mum and Dad go?' Danny asked. The wooden ball – they'd lost the plastic one so long ago no one could even remember it – rattled back and forth in a feverish mid-field tango. The score stood at 6–4 to Zoë. Ben played with furious concentration. He *had* to get even or die.

'What time did Mum and Dad go?' Danny asked again, loudly.

''Bout quarter to nine. They said they'd be late tonight.' Ali pressed her head against the window and tried to probe the darkness outside. They were pretty spooky-feeling, somehow, the shapes made by things in the garden. She pulled the curtains tight and pushed Danny's leg with her foot. 'So what's *Dead Wreckers* about?'

'*Dead Reckoning*,' Danny corrected. 'It's that thing, you know, with dead birds and stuff on a boat? That thing with Tod Ellman in it?'

'No,' Ali said, 'I don't know.'

'There's axes,' said Danny, 'plus a crossbow. Plus this mad guy hangs birds round his neck?'

'Dead or alive?'

'What?'

'The birds round his neck.'

'Dead, of course – *ner*. What did you think?'

'Dead birds,' said Ali. 'Great,' said Ali. 'I knew I should've come with you.'

'I suppose *you* could've got something better.'

'Not *better*. . .' Ali hesitated. 'Not *scary*.'

'Scary.' Ben snorted. 'Like something from Stu Smethick's Video Vaults is *scary*.'

Danny said, 'Some of them are. Did you see *Living Dead*? Wish I hadn't. It was gross.'

He dimmed the lights and set up the tape. The table football ended noisily at last, Ben the winner by a single goal half deliberately let in by Zoë, to save them having to play again – and again – until Ben won.

Danny looked up. 'Where's Jamie, then?'

Three heavy knocks at the door brought Danny to his feet. He had time to catch Ali's eye before Jamie Prentice burst in behind a tray of top grub and a stupid grin that took in Danny's expression. Jamie set down his tray. 'I got Chipsticks, popcorn, Bloaters. Coke and Oasis to drink.' He looked around at them. 'What?'

'Nothing,' Danny said, darkly. 'Only don't knock three times that way.'

Jamie put on a stupid voice. 'Why – will something happen?'

'They knocked three times in *Living Dead*,' Zoë said, helpfully. 'Before they picked out their eyes.'

'Yuk.'

'Gross.'

'Evil.'

'Relax.' Jamie said. 'Can we go for it now?'

Danny pressed Play. The first four trailers advertised standard thrillers with many explosions and the usual gravelly voice-over. Danny reckoned the man with the gravelly voice did all right from video trailers. Ben said he probably put the voice on specially, but Zoë reckoned he sounded that way all the time. Probably he sounded that way when he asked for the Shreddies at breakfast. Danny tried putting on a gravelly voice through the cushion Zoë threw at him. *They never knew Shreddies could cost them an arm and a leg until they asked the wild man to pass them. Your worst nightmare. Dad, first thing in the morning. Guess who's coming to breakfast.* Danny was still trying out his gravelly voice when the credits for *Dead Reckoning* came up – dark credits, with a brooding, tension-filled soundtrack. An eye. A boat. A starlit sea. Then the titles. Anna Pirsig. Tod Ellman. *Dead Reckoning.* Directed by Vita Corrollis.

'Is this an eighteen?' Zoë shifted uncomfortably.

Danny said, 'Nope.' Then he said, 'I don't *think* so.'

'Shreddies.' Ali got up. 'You shouldn't have mentioned Shreddies just now. I might have to go and get some.'

'Oh, sit down,' Zoë said irritably. 'You don't need Shreddies with all this stuff on the table.'

Ali sat down. *Dead Reckoning* opened dramatically and continued that way with no let-up. A couple of neat surprises brought everyone's heart to their mouth. Everyone drew gradually – almost imperceptibly – closer together without noticing. Ali looked behind her two or three times. No one ate anything much after the accident with the boat-hook. Jamie got up and closed the door. 'Ber!' he went, grabbing Ali before he sat down. Ali jumped out of her skin. 'Jamie! You prat! *Never do that again!*'

The plot had opened out fairly predictably. It didn't take a genius to see that a yacht plus a wholesome-looking couple plus a madman, all at sea together, added up to an edge-of-the-seat gripper. Everyone knew what was coming, but it never failed to surprise them. They were a good third of the way through the action before the tension became unbearable. Already the madman calling himself the Ancient Mariner had hacksawed his way out of the cabin he was locked in and shot an albatross with his crossbow and left it – the albatross, not the crossbow – in the kitchen of the wholesome-looking couple about to enjoy their yacht trip. Already three minor characters had lost out to major explosions, plus the guy with the forgettable face you *know* is going to get killed right from the start was about to get *his*, big time, when Ali said, 'Can't we have a Pause?'

'Good decision.' Ben got up and stretched his arms.

'Listen.' Zoë listened. 'What's that noise outside?'

Jamie parted the curtains. ''S only a catfight next door.'

Ali shuddered. 'Bizarre. Sounds like someone's crying.'

'Haven't you heard a cat-fight before? They sound really freaky sometimes. Probably facing each other out. Probably go on for ages.'

'I don't like it,' Zoë said. 'Can't we make them stop?'

Jamie opened the window. 'Hey! Cats! Cool it!' He turned and grinned. 'That do you?'

'Are you going to Pause the film, or what? Here, let me.' Ali hit Pause, and BBC2 flickered up. She wished they could stay with *What's My Garden? What's My Garden?* was comforting.

Something hit the window hard. Jamie closed it quickly. 'Hey,' he said, 'what was *that*?'

'A bat or something,' Zoë said, glad he'd closed the window anyway. 'There's bats and stuff in the garden.'

'Bats never fly into windows,' Ben said. 'Their radar's too good for that.'

'Probably it's a bird.' Danny looked wired. 'Probably an albatross. Probably there's an albatross out in the kitchen, probably going to –'

'Danny! Shut up!' Ali flung down a cushion. 'That's it. I'm getting the Shreddies.'

Ali marched out. Zoë dashed out after her. Ben followed a moment later. Jamie looked as though he wanted to. After a minute, he did. 'Might as well join the queue.'

'What queue?'

'Bog-break. I thought that's why we Paused.'

'Leave me here with bats an' stuff getting in at the windows, why don't you?' Danny shouted after him, mentally calculating the distance down the corridor –

quite a way – from the living room to the loo. '*Can't you go to the bog on your own or something?*'

Everyone came back on edge. First the lights were too bright. Then Ben had all the cushions. Then no one was prepared to go back out to the kitchen cupboard to fetch the Twiglets. Then Zoë, last back from the loo, insisted Danny be prised from prime place on the settee to let someone *else* take a turn, she didn't care who, so long as it wasn't Danny. Finally Jamie farted, but no one would open any windows. At last the room settled. Zoë hit Play. *Dead Reckoning* jumped back onscreen. This time the soundtrack was different – enhanced, somehow, by the banging sound everyone had tried so hard to ignore. But it was no use. The intermittent banging upstairs that everyone had heard clearly for some time seemed more insistent every minute. So the wind had got up outside. The widows were closed – weren't they? What *was* that banging upstairs?

'Hear it?' Ali listened. 'Maybe a window's blown open?'

Danny said, 'Pass the Coke.'

'Danny. Something's banging.'

Danny topped up his glass. 'So?'

'It'll only go *on* banging, won't it?'

'So fix it.'

'You.'

After a moment Danny got up reluctantly. 'Coming with me, then?'

'It's only upstairs.'

'Correct.'

'So go and see what it *is*.'

Danny appealed to Zoë. 'Coming with me, Zo? Only as far as the bathroom?'

Zoë hit Volume ruthlessly. 'You should've gone when everyone else went.'

'Well, I wouldn't mind going now.'

Zoë turned to look at him. 'Want me to hold your hand?'

'I'm going.'

'So go.'

'I'm *going*.'

'So *go*.'

Zoë turned back to *Dead Reckoning*. Tod Ellman was really in trouble. A major problem with his fishing line meant Tod – or Bob, as Tod's character was called – might even get dragged overboard. Shark fishing from the deck of his yacht, wholesome-looking Bob had hooked something bigger than he'd ever hooked before.

Shreddievision

The yacht cut swiftly through the water as Bob fought to reel in his catch. Down in the galley, Bob's wife made coffee. Tension built with the soundtrack. Bob struggled gamely on deck, his line strained, the music built, Bob's wife perked, Bob fought, the water threshed – and something, something *big* was rising on that fishing line, something big and dark and –

Danny said, 'So who's coming with me, then? Just as far as the bathroom.'

Wholesome Bob fought with his line. The big dark something-or-other rose up steadily through the water towards him, and it wasn't, ever, in a million years, going to be a – cut to Bob's wife, knocking over a pot of hot coffee in horrified slow motion – back to Bob – it wasn't ever, in a million years, going to be a *fish* –

'Haven't you *gone* yet?' Zoë snapped, terminally irritated. '*Go* to the loo if you want to.'

'I just am.'

'So stop going on and *on*.'

'What's it to you?' Danny squirmed in his seat. 'I'll go in a minute, all right?'

The drowned-looking Ancient Mariner surfaced beside the yacht *Wedding Guest* and made a lunge for the hand-rail. Slowly, he removed Bob's hook from his clothes with a twisted smile on his face. He could only come in where invited, and here was his invite on board. Slowly, he hauled himself up. He landed one leg, then two, on deck. He watched Wholesome Bob reel in his slack line. Then he slithered below. Wholesome Bob scratched his head. Where had that big fish *gone* to? Cut to Bob's wife – Anna Pirsig – mopping up coffee in the galley. She looks up: 'That you, Bob?' Was that a sound on the stair?

'What about that banging upstairs?' Ali said, suddenly. 'It sounds like it's banging in my room.'

'So why don't you go up and see?' Danny asked her, irritably.

'I thought *you* were.' said Ali.

'He's scared something'll jump out and grab him,' Ben said, looking pretty jumpy himself. 'He's scared an albatross'll swim up the toilet and bite him.'

'Ha.' Danny said, 'you're so funny. Stop me laughing my head off.'

Anna Pirsig finished up in the galley. The cookpots banged together as the yacht rode a gathering storm. As Anna looked up she caught sight of a shape behind the door, something wet and dark and drowned-looking, *with a dead bird around its neck*. The Ancient Mariner pushed wide the galley door. Anna's hand closed around a kitchen knife. Slowly she turned around.

'Want a Shreddie?' Ali's eyes were out on stalks.

Jamie twitched. 'No thanks, I'm stuffed.'

'I mean to look through, not eat.'

'To *look* through? How d'you mean?'

'Like this,' Ali explained, eyeing the screen with difficulty through a square of malted cereal. 'You can't see particularly well through 'em, which is good, 'cos it's just what you want. Plus you can tilt them – like this – and then you *can't see anything at all.*'

Jamie looked helpless. 'How is that good?'

'Good for bad bits,' said Zoë.

'This one's OK,' said Ali, squinting like mad through her Shreddie as Anna's knife flashed onscreen. 'They're all slightly different – some you can't see anything through.'

'If you keep 'em straight, they're OK.'

Zoë helped herself from the cereal packet. 'If you tilt 'em slightly, you can block out stuff really quick. This one's good – you can still see through the top corner to check when the bad bits are over.'

'Shreddievision,' said Ali. 'Blocks out the bits you don't need to see. You should try it some time. We always watch *bad* films through Shreddies.'

Fever Dreams

Something rumbled overhead. Danny leapt to his feet.

'Did you hear *that*?' Ali dropped her Shreddie. Danny looked a bit green.

'That's major,' Zoë considered the ceiling. 'Something *big* falling over.'

Ali hit Pause, and Wholesome Bob froze. They all sat in jangled silence, the hiss of the wind outside lifting the curtains very slightly. Jamie went on eating crisps. Ali snatched them away.

PEE – PEE – PEE – PEE – PEE – PEE –

'The smoke detector!' Zoë jumped up.

PEE – PEE – PEE –

Danny said, 'How *can* it be?'

PEE – PEE –

'What happens is, something burns and smoke goes in the detector, then it senses it, THEN IT BEEPS, OK?'

'I mean – who left something on?'

'Don't look at *me*.' Ali said, 'I never even –'

'What's it *matter* who did it? Let's just go out an' *stop* it –'

PEE – PEE – PEE –

'What is it? What's going on?' Jamie scratched his head.

Shreddievision

'Did you just wake up or something?'

'Haven't you ever heard a smoke alarm before?'

PEE – PEE – PEE – PEE – PEE –

Ali flipped unexpectedly. *'I can't stand it! Get me a chair!'*

Danny got Ali a chair to stand on. Then he opened the door. The amount of smoke filling the corridor surprised everyone, until Zoë dimly remembered she'd made toast – or at least *put bread in the toaster* – long ago enough to forget about it completely and *way* before Wholesome Bob reeled in the Ancient Mariner, which was much the same thing. And how was *she* supposed to know it'd go and get stuck in the toaster and fill the whole house with an acrid smell like a million burning socks?

'It's just,' Danny said bitterly, out in the garden, 'it's just your luck it *isn't* burning socks.'

By the time Ali'd stood on a chair and killed the alarm and they'd opened the windows and doors and wafted out as much smoke as possible and gathered together in the garden, much of what had happened before the alarm had gone off, temporarily forgotten, had begun to filter back.

Ali considered the open windows and doors. 'Great. Now the whatever-it-is can get in.'

'The what?' Ben asked.

'The bat-thing, or whatever it was, that hit the window earlier.'

'What about that thump we heard? Like something big falling over?' Danny turned his eyes upstairs. '*Maybe it got in already.*'

Zoë swallowed. There were worse things than thumps in the house. One of them was leaving a good film unfinished. If Anna Pirsig had the nerve to face out a dripping wet lunatic in a galley kitchen with not enough room to swing a – to swing an *albatross*, then she, Zoë Pearsall, had the nerve to watch her do it, even if it *was* through a Shreddie.

Zoë set her chin. 'Well, I've had about enough of standing around freezing to death in the garden. I'm going in to watch the rest of the film, and I don't care *what* happens next.'

'If it wasn't for your stupid toast we wouldn't even *be* in the garden,' Ali shouted bitterly, marching in after her all the same. Jamie followed slowly, his back slightly less unconcerned-looking than it usually was. The night's drama was getting to him, Danny could tell.

Danny said, 'Let's all go up and sort it. All together, I mean.'

'Sort what?' Ben asked.

'That thing upstairs. Might as well get it over with.'

'I suppose,' Ben said. 'Might as well. So long as the others'll come.'

Danny led the way. After some – considerable – persuasion, Ali and Zoë followed. Ben and Jamie brought up the rear, Jamie wishing he wasn't. The tension built as they climbed the darkened staircase. After a fiercely whispered discussion they'd decided *not* to put on the light, so as not to annoy the whatever-it-was in the bedroom. The whatever-it-was in the bedroom had sounded really quite large.

Danny peered around the corner of Ali's bedroom's darkened door. He swept the room with his *Mission Impossible* gun-hand. Then he snapped on the light.

"S'okay,' he said, 'nothing in here. ''Cept millions of stuff Ali has.'

Ali's room showed every sign of Ali, but no sign whatever of heavy objects falling over, or – which was more worrying – *heavy objects jumping in*. With the Ancient Mariner's creepy climb into Wholesome Bob's yacht uppermost in everyone's mind, Danny turned to the Olds' room. He pushed Zoë forward. 'Your turn.'

'I don't think so,' Zoë side-stepped neatly.

'Hear that?' said Ali. 'Whatever it is, it's *in here*.'

'Your turn, Ben.' Zoë pushed him.

'Go for it, Ben.'

'Yeah, right.'

Reluctantly, Ben Prentice pushed wide the darkened door of his best mate's parents' bedroom. Inside it, the blinds banged annoyingly in the wind hissing in through the window. The only blind that *didn't* bang was the one hitched up on a lump. A largish lump, in the middle of the floor, not unlike a –

'What is it?' hissed Danny. 'What's in there?'

– a largish lump, in the middle of the floor, *not unlike a body*.

'I don't know,' Ben said. 'Something.'

'Like what?' Zoë wanted to know.

Jamie said, 'Is it a dead body?'

Ben considered the question, as though the answer to it could be too much for Jamie to understand. Then he nodded slowly. 'Could be. Take a look. There's something under the window.'

Ali wished they had Shreddies to look through. She didn't want to see anything that she wouldn't be able to forget. Following Danny, one by one, they skirted the lump on the floor.

Shreddievision

The lump didn't groan or moan. It didn't jump up and leave dead birds or knives in the kitchen.

It didn't move or breathe. It wouldn't ever move or breathe, mainly because it was a lampstand.

Ben snapped on the light in disgust. 'Typical.' He snorted.

After Danny had righted the heavy chrome-and-frosted-glass lampstand that a flapping blind had somehow floored in the Olds' room, and Ben had helped him do it, Ben wiped his hands on his jeans and looked around in a what's-next kind of way. He pulled down the sleeves of his sweater. Then he looked at Jamie. 'We're going home now,' he said. 'Right, Jamie?'

'It's never anything *good* like they find in films,' Jamie whined. 'It's always jus' something *boring*. That's always jus' what it is.'

'Yeah, well,' Danny said, 'it's my house. Go and find something disgusting in yours, why don't you?'

The Prentice boys thought they might. Danny watched them go – they only lived just round the corner – with a feeling he'd rather go with them than rejoin his sisters in the House of Smoke and Shreddies and Things That Went Bump in the Night. Not to mention the

Olds. The Olds would have to come back at *some* point. Then they'd kick up a fuss.

When Danny re-entered the living room he found both his sisters had tuned in like mad to Shreddievision. After a while he tuned in himself. The end of *Dead Reckoning* somehow made more sense through a haze of malted cereal. If only life could be viewed through Shreddievision. It might look better that way. They should have glasses made. Except life wasn't much like a film. Instead of bits that were too bad to see, mostly things were just boring. Except for things like famine and war. It'd take a lot more than Shreddievision to make famine and war look better.

Tap. Tap. Tap.

'*What was that?*' Danny sat up. The hairs on the back of his neck stood up – he could practically *hear* them doing it.

Tap. Tap. Tap. Three knocks. On the window. Just like *in Living Dead.* Before the Undead come. The Undead always tapped. It let you know they were coming.

Tap. Tap. Tap.

'Who's there?' Zoë called, like she wanted to know. Not someone with birds round their *neck.* Not someone, she hoped, *who left a pool of water where they were standing.*

'Someone's out there.'

'*Who?*' Ali asked them, whitely.

'The thing from *Living Dead*, I 'spect,' Danny said, getting a clue. 'Prob'ly the thing from *Living Dead* that waits till you're fast asleep, then it comes an' picks out your eyes.'

Zoë ripped open the curtains. A horribly distorted face with exploded, slug-like lips waited against the glass outside. Zoë recoiled. Quick as a snake, she opened the window and shouted '*Ben Prentice! That's not very funny!*'

After *Dead Reckoning* had finally finished up with Wholesome Bob and his wife sailing away into the sunset over an ocean covered in tiny bits of blown-up Ancient Mariner, Danny dashed upstairs. He checked the windows in the Olds' room – closed tightly now against the wind – then he dashed back down again with sleeping bags, which he gave out so he had the best one.

After the film they watched snooker. After snooker, they watched a late-night thriller involving Charles Bronson and stolen hospital patients. As the celebrity interview after *that* flickered over the wrecked and

Fever Dreams

bombshelled living room, Danny and Zoë and Alison Pearsall lay done up like pupae or caterpillars, each in a sleeping bag, each watching Shreddievision far into the night, until one by one, they fell asleep. They didn't even wake up when the key turned in the front door and the Olds tiptoed quietly to bed, sniffing the burnt-smelling air, smothering whispers as they went.

If you've recovered from

Fever Dreams

look out for more Tales from a Sick Bed . . .

The Medicine Chest

You know when you're ill in bed, and everything
looks larger than life, kind of super-real and
out-of-scale, as though something as big as a gorilla
in the wardrobe is about to reveal itself?

Open the Medicine Chest!

Brainstorms

You're hot – very hot. You know when you're off
school and ill in bed, and everything seems kind
of large and nightmarish – when your brain
dips out and explores strange ideas and the
wallpaper hurts your eyes?

That's a Brainstorm!

Warning! Read these stories and the world will
never look the same again.

Will Dudgeon is thirteen years old when his body is stolen by a century-hopping villain. Suddenly Will's the oldest man he's ever seen (with all the aches and pains that go with that).

At least he's inherited the right job. As assistant at Nettlefold and Dad Funeral Directors, Will can offer really wicked, wedged, full-on, top-dog, superfine funerals, best and plushest on the terrace!

But for how long? Can Will persuade the dastardly Hornbeam to give him his young body back or will his next funeral be his own?